THE AMY JOHNSON COLLECTION OF ESSAYS

TOP FLIGHT - LAKENHEATH AND GARVOCHLEAH - ANGUS

Amy Johnson

authorHOUSE°

AuthorHouse™ UK
1663 Liberty Drive
Bloomington, IN 47403 USA
www.authorhouse.co.uk
Phone: 0800.197.4150

Published by AuthorHouse   08/09/2016

ISBN: 978-1-5246-6091-8 (sc)
ISBN: 978-1-5246-6090-1 (hc)
ISBN: 978-1-5246-6092-5 (e)

Print information available on the last page.

ESSAY ONE
TOP FLIGHT-
RAF *Lakenheath*

*This short essay is dedicated to the final flight of
USAF Fast Jet Pilot –RAF Lakenheath_*

INDEX

PART I
FALCON LAKENHEATH

RADIO CALL

For a brief moment, Major Thom, Falcon as his friends called him, hesitated, and then he radioed control tower to clear him for takeoff. He glanced through the cockpit canopy of his fast jet at the surrounding English countryside. The day lay ahead brilliant, sunny and crisp beneath the shimmering sun.

Behind him, lay the airfields of the Royal Air Force base at Lakenheath, and beyond a green fence, he could see other fighters lined up along the runway, for takeoff; soon returning back to the United States after the end of hostilities in the Middle East.

The US Air force was finally disbanding its jets from the RAF base in Lakenheath, where they had been stationed for some time.

Ahead of him, as he waited for instructions from ground control, was the runway itself, the darkest black tarmac, flanked by twin rows of switched off lights, while the sun illuminated his path clearly, as it had done many times before? Behind him, there were humped banks of glittering snow, which the snow plow blades had pushed aside. To the left was the control tower, standing like a citadel glowing and shining brilliantly among the many hangars.

He could see the radiomen and women, busy on their stations as night was approaching. He watched them and knew that there was warmth and merriment, the staff waiting for his departure and then heading off to their cars, waiting for the normal night shift to take over.

There were the parties in the mess. The lights in the huddled hangars were being switched off one by one and the bitter night would soon creep upon, the fighter jets, the fuel trucks and the station lights would come on, with a brilliant orange red hue and flood its airfields.

For tonight there were no, wandering aviators looking down, checking their bearings – the Christmas parties in full swing and with only one young pilot making a trip over the North Sea and back making sure all systems were operating at speed.

There was no hurry and the watch read clearly, in the dim neon blue glow, of the control panel, where the rows of dials seemed to shimmer, quiver and dance. He loved his warm, smug cockpit making sure there were no icing; he turned up the heating buttons. His feet cocooned, rested, safe and warm, shielded by the cold outside – while he would begin his sortie at 600 miles an hour.

"Echo, Oscar, Delta …)

The controller's voice quickly broke over the headphone, almost as if he was in the cockpit, beside him as his co-pilot.

'Echo, Oscar Delta ….control replied

"Echo, Oscar, cleared for takeoff,' he said.

Falcon responded by easing the throttle forward, holding the jet steady, down the airfield's marked lines. The engine roared with a startling whine, then revved up into a loud usual thunder.

The jet moved quickly and in no time, the flashing lights were a fading continuous blur. The jet rose and the nose wheel lost contact with the runway and then there was silence as the noises settled down. The main wheels came away and their rumblings ceased. The speed built up till the jet was flying at some knots, heading for a given direction. The runway flashed passed, as the jet gently climbed, turning to the right and gradually eased the undercarriage lever as it did so.

Beneath and behind him, all that could be seen was an empty bay, as the jet propelled forward and the undercarriage disappeared from view. The dashboard lights representing the wheels extinguished themselves. The jet began to climb.

'Echo, Oscar, Delta – cleared airfield – all set,' Falcon radioed to control.

Echo Oscar Delta – over to you the controller said, then Falcon quickly switched channels.

The Lossiemouth channel air control frequency was busy, but then contact was made. Falcon knew the map by heart, although he had the map course to hand, if he missed it. Soon he was over the North Sea, after 50 minutes of flying time. Falcon radioed the control to give him a steer. He followed instructions and this brought him to descend. All the procedures were routine, there was 80 minutes of fuel still left.

LOSSIEMOUTH

Gradually he straightened up and settled into a steady course, and straight ahead the instructions were clear. The jet rose straight outwards to growing black velvet of a black sky, stars began to flicker brilliantly as the night grew darker. Below the map of Scotland was growing smaller as her pine forests were layered with white snow fields around them. A village or two glittered with twinkling lights. The carol singers would be out in full, Christmas was the same wherever it was celebrated, the language was different but the sentiment was the same.

From Lossiemouth, Falcon knew he could get a lift down to Leuchers and then he would return to Lakenheath in the morning, after a night's rest at the base.

His altimeter read 30,000 feet; he eased his nose forward, and noted his air speed was 400 knots.

Below him, the Scottish border would be appearing in 20 minutes. He would soon be landing.

Once over the North Sea, he became aware of a booming sound, then a sound of silence, followed by the booming sound. He quickly looked at the dashboard, and could not see anything across. Suddenly he realized the compass was stuck and so was the backup – something must have jarred it. Normally the systems were 100 percent reliable, but it was not uncommon – the purpose of his solo trip. In any event, he would call Leuchers or Lossiemouth in a few minutes and they would give him a ground controlled approach – and he would be given a safe passage. He glanced at his watch, and before trying Leuchers, the right procedure would be to inform Control - tower did not respond, to which he was tuned if there was a problem.

CONTROL

Echo sierra Delta – come in control. He stopped, there was no continuing – there was no response. He tried a few times more. Same result. So the radio too was jammed or dead. Control tower did not respond.

DREAD

Fighting the rising sense of dread, terror, fear and panic – he was now in a situation that could be lethal or fatal, he swallowed hard and a sudden calm took over. He slowly took in a sharp breath.

Then he switched to Lossiemouth frequency and tried to wake up Lossie ahead of him lay the beautiful Scottish countryside, sitting sedately in her ever green forests of green pines, and its Ground controlled approach system supreme for bringing home lost pilots. On this channel, the radio was silent. He tried other known channels, nothing. His breath and muttering reflected back to him. The steady sound of his engine was reassuring. It was a solitary place, over Scotland's North Sea. Being alone, in a fast jet, surrounded by steel with lofty wings could be lonely and equally terrifying. His jet continued to blaze through the lit sky, throwing out more than a thousand horses per second, if not more. But the loneliness was not offset by the knowledge his jet was fully functional except for the fact, that he was now unable to speak to men or women or any of the many network stations around the world – his transmission systems were down – he was unable to contact them, so much help and yet not a single streak of light on his dashboard. The control towers were all linked, and could locate his position via multiple GPS systems. The radar operators should be able to detect him, although he could not contact them – help would soon be sent. He longed for a sound to break through 'Echo Sierra Delta – we have you - and then they would begin to guide him down.

He tried transmitting again – hoping a one way transmission would work. The USAF had taken two years to train him to fly the fighters and most of the time had been spent in training for emergency procedures – the whole point was to stay calm in an emergency and not panic. There were millions of scenarios to safety that he could quick scan through his memory files. His training began to take effect.

DASHBOARD

His eyes quickly scanned the dash board and the instruments were all working except the compass and the radio – that was no coincidence. Something had happened to the circuits and they were linked somehow. He tried to take stock of the nature of his dilemma. He decided to reduce the throttle setting to a lower one, to maintain maximum flight stability and ultimately longevity.

He recalled the many times he had heard it recanted not to waste valuable fuel. Reducing power setting from higher revs to lower always did the trick. It would enable him to stay in the air, should he need it. He eased the throttle and kept a keen eye on the revs, - he felt his jet slow down, the nose rising fractionally – so he adjusted the flight trim and kept her straight and absolutely level.

The instruments were behaving, the airspeed, the altimeter, vertical speed indicator – were all sound. He watched his left and right banking and skidding across the sky – everything was fine. It was perfectly new to find a place to land his jet with his functioning instruments and judge the best he could with his navigational aids. Conditions of brilliant weather helped, to navigate a fast moving jet, using the eyes, to identify some land known mark, a cathedral or distinctive building. At night it was possible but extremely difficult.

PATTERNS

The only thing were familiar patterns. Edinburgh looked different from Aberdeen and so did Lossiemouth and Leuchers. He knew these cities well and especially Leuchers and Lossiemouth. He could identify the coast line and he knew the fighter airfield, whose red indicator beacon would be blipping continuously, giving its morse identification. He would land safely he was sure of that. He began to let the jet down slowly toward the coast line, his mind feverishly looking ahead and reducing speed.

His watch showed him how much time had lapsed – he glanced around and saw a searchlight in the sky and was relieved. As he slipped toward Lossie, the sense of others gripped him with hope. All the elements seemed to be supporting him – the stars seemed to shine impressively with an uncanny brilliance; no more emitting a sparkling hostility like before. The stratospheric temperature was unaltered; below him lay his only enemy – the brutal North sea – waiting to swallow up any unwary lost fighter pilot. And yet at 10,000 feet and still lowering the jet he realized that the ink black sea – was all he could see – the moon reflecting endlessly on an endless sea. The Scottish Haar seemed to be coming in.

As he flew westwards a breeze was springing up – then it began to gather speed. Coming in contact with a winter ground, the moisture in the air had vaporized and formed a thick fog. He had no idea how far it would stretch and without a radio, he could soon become lost over unfamiliar territory. He had no option but to find a safe landing ground in Scotland or Norway, whichever was closer. His eyes guided him as best as they could, -it was a question of landing this jet.

At 10,000 feet, he pulled out of his dive, increasing power, but being careful not to waste precious fuel. He recalled quickly the instructions of his flight commanders.

If the cloud did not break soon, he would have to also consider bailing out as an option. His ejector seat was sound, and there had been no incidents, when it could have failed him.

His first move would be then to turn the jet toward open ocean away from all human habitation – that was a flight safety discipline well indoctrinated into him, since his early flying days. Town's people were to be avoided at all costs as were schools, children's facilities and domestic homes – he was sure he was in no danger of this at all. The procedures were entrenched and drilled into his head. He would not last in the cold frozen North Sea, even when supported by his yellow life jacket, even if his ditching was picked up by helicopters minutes away. Ditching was the last resort procedure in extreme emergencies. All aircraft approaching any of the UK coasts would be readily visible on radar scanners – and their early warning systems. Jets would be scrambled immediately if his behavior was considered threatening or out of the ordinary – 'An aircraft in distress.'

PROCEDURES

The radio scanners had their input procedures to follow when warned by odd form of behavior. If his transponder had not been picked up, as suspicious activity in an age or terror would certainly give them a wakeup call. Jets moving out to sea or flying in small triangles – fast and haphazardly is intended to send out a distress signal or to attract urgent attention.

The controller is often informed and jets are scrambled in a hurry. The hope was that the other aircraft if he came across any would have a radio and could send out a rescue call.

These were some of his options, and he needed a bit of luck on his side. These were desperate measures to be taken in desperate times. Hoping for a reserve aircraft to lead him to a safe place or landing site was now only a prayer. He glanced sideways he had half an hour of fuel left. His fuel looked healthy and he decided to commence, emergency maneuvers. After a few moments he did another emergency performance – ten minutes later, he saw and noticed nothing. He began to pray slowly, something he had not done in a very long time and hoped someone would find him. He started to panic – the fuel would not hold out forever – he began to speak urgently into the dead microphone – a few seconds later his breathing became strained – he felt sad that no one could rescue him. He looked out at the horizon, the fog and the total darkness below him. He would have to bail out there was no other option – he would try one final triangle – and then he would bail out.

SCRAMBLED FAST JETS

Suddenly he saw a shadow – an outline of a plane – he thought he was hallucinating, but as he looked closer, he realized it was another aircraft, coming towards him through the thickest of fogs. It began signaling to him, and did a small circle. He could not believe it, they must have heard the radio – it was only half dead – dysfunctional but not completely out – his screams were heard on the other side and they had begun to edge towards him.

Suddenly Falcon, saw four jets appear, they had been scrambled. They too were beside him in no time at all. Then he realized what had happened.

It was typical in military aviation, scrambling Jets was the act of quickly getting Jets airborne to react to an immediate threat, usually to intercept enemy aircraft. The Jets came up right beside, him, and seeing he was one of their own, saluted, letting him know that they knew he was in distress, and they would get him down to safety.

His odd behavior had been picked up on radar and they were taking no chances. One Jet came right beside Falcon and stayed there firmly. The Angels on fire was a code name used for them and unidentified aircraft like his were known as bogeys- while known ones were bandits. He they had confirmed was neither. The scramble ordered to alert had saved his life. Their airspace had been penetrated, and fighter squadrons must have been on quick reaction alert – a QRA and their crews had taken off within minutes – they may have suspected a Russian jet – as many had been known to venture into British airspace of late. The transponder too would have been picked up by them, the beacon transmitting a crisis frequency.

The Jet kept turning and then one came flying towards him – He swung his left hand wing tip and then he was beside him. The other three Jets kept a safe distance behind him. The Jet aircraft was completing a circle and turning. He began to climb to his height and take up station on his left wing tip. He was trying to keep up to fly beside falcon, but he could not keep up with the jet. It was hard to believe it was another aircraft moving his way up – and then he would disappear in the fog. Falcon eased his throttle back and began to edge towards him. He kept turning and then he began to fly towards him. He swung his left hand wing tip and then suddenly he was beside him, and lined to fly in formation. His jet flew next to his and Falcon could clearly make out the Pilot's shadow, shape and form.

He could fly at Falcon's speed and he had been scrambled to assist him down.

He held station alongside Falcon, then banked gently to the left; beckoning Falcon to keep formation with him. Then he swung sharply through 180 degrees and straightened up and began leading toward the Scottish coast and once out of the fog and thick cloud formation; Falcon could see him well. He then noticed that the Met office had released samples of the upper atmosphere – and given data of weather forecasts. The jet was flying as though in a display of sorts or even in the mode of a fly-past, heroic, as if attracting gasps from a waiting crowd, bringing home an ailing aircraft.

Inside his cockpit, Falcon could make him out, his outline and his helmet as he waved out of his side window, reassuring him. He raised his hand pointed downward twice, signaling clearly till he grasped what he was saying to him.

He jabbed his fingers forward and down, asking him to formate with him. Falcon nodded, quickly and struck his left hand point forward with one finger, - then waving his hand.

Falcon noticed his fuel would not last long and gave a visual indication that his fuel did not have long before his engine would cut out. The Pilot nodded – then he slowly began to head out of the fog of dark clouds.

He increased his speed and then he was beside him again. Soon they were now heading fast forward – over the shrouded lands of Scotland. Falcon glanced at the altimeter they were 2000 feet and diving. The other Jets were no longer visible as Falcon focused on the Jet ahead of him with full concentration.

The fog was thick on the ground but with thinner parts enabling a plane to land easily without Ground controlled approach assistance. Falcon could only imagine the flood of instructions being released from the radar to the pilot next to him– the wind was around 300 knots between them. Falcon kept his eyes on him, formatting as precisely as he could and watching all his hand and light signals. He marveled at his luck and the masterful performance of his helper. Then he signaled to Falcon, to lower his undercarriage. Falcon moved his level forward and downward, till he heard the wheels come down. He sighed and smiled happily. The Pilot ahead of him pointed down again – another descent was coming – and the letter J S was painted on his jet – probably his call sign – then they descended and gently this time.

DESCENT

He leveled out then went into a circular turn. He knew his fuel gauge would be ready to zero out in some few minutes. The Pilot realized that there was serious danger and moved quickly.

Falcon's sweat broke out behind his neck – if only he would hurry – he hoped for his sake he knew what he was doing. Then he straightened out – and signaled a dive signal – Falcon followed in a flat descent – from a height of no more than 150 feet.

Passing through a dim lit sky, he could see nothing but grey – the visibility was down to zero, no shape or substance could be discerned. Now fifty feet away, he could see the Pilot flying with absolute certainty towards a goal. Falcon could not make out what it was. His lights were turned down as they could be treacherous and hallucinations could be invoked by staring for too long at a fog – Pilots had become mesmerized. He was a professional and was guiding him supremely well.

Keeping up with him, Falcon eased back, as the Pilot pointed, at him then forward through the windscreen – which read fly on now and land safely.

TOUCHDOWN

Falcon, nodded, and saw the runway – he focused hard, with a slight bang - the Pilot touched down, and there was the rumble of two jets landing at the same time. The wheels held – while the Jet stopped ahead of him.

The lights on either side of the runway were moving slower and slower.

The Jet stopped. Falcon found his hands clenched squeezing the brake inwards. He held onto it for ages – not believing he had stopped and was safe. He finally released the brake – then turned off the engine – the fuel gauge was now almost on zero – they would have to tow the fighter – the systems all slowly switched off.

He unwrapped himself from the seat and parachute and pack. The jet ahead of Falcon, then roared into motion was gone, waving as he did so. He acknowledged.

Falcon watched the Jet leave the other three joined him, the angels of fire ; no doubt other assignments were calling, from which they had taken a short detour to confront or to save him. The control tower trucks were alongside him in no time at all, the fire truck, ambulance and half a dozen other vehicles were all on ready stand by. They all stood there for ten minutes or so. Their headlights came on, while he simply sat there frozen. A voice shouted, 'Hello there.'

RECEPTION

Falcon stepped out of the cockpit, jumped out from the jet's wing straight onto the tarmac and hurried towards the lights. An air force officer came forward and shook Falcon's hands.

'Good landing, given the circumstances –Sir.'

'Yes, quite extraordinary, yes – Falcon said.

He was grateful once he was led into a warm car and happy to be alive.

'We will run to the officers mess Sir,' said the junior RAF officer.

'Sure, I will be grateful for the warmth of the place and am sure grateful to be alive.'

The car passed a taxi rank, then the control tower, some more mess buildings. As it moved away from the airfield, they went past some snow filled fields at the end of the runway.

'You were lucky Sir,' the officer said.

'You did not run out of fuel, having been lost in the thick clouds and fog.'

'Yes, that was damned lucky,' he agreed. 'I did run out just past the landing.'

'Well my radio failed for starters.'

'Wow.'

'Yes?'

'Quite something – and no compass – flying is absolutely impossible in these conditions, that are to say without the key instruments.'

'Then the Jets found you?' he said matter of fact.

'Yes, somehow they found me; I will have to find out how?'

'Must be the emergency procedures you conducted Sir, there was some chat at the base – about them.'

'I see, they were picked up by the team.'

Falcon shrugged – 'Good thing too!'

'Yes Sir – we are almost there now.'

They drove in silence – while Falcon let all the information sink in.'

'Sir, RAF Lossiemouth, just around the corner sir.'

'Operational base – is also not far Sir, this is near a storage depot Sir.'

'I have heard,' he responded politely.

'Excuse me Sir.'

He stopped the car and got out.

The Mess was there, with some flight and some navigational huts not far from it.

The lights were on, and some men came out.

'Sir, welcome you have made it safely from the air base.'

'Yes, thank you,' Falcon's mind was whirling, hurting and he was not wanting to give a full logical explanation.

The Mess was the usual.

The procedure was the same – He was shown into a seating area while they brought him a drink, the hall was spacious but a bit out of date. It had obviously seen better days. There were two leather club chairs – and the cloakroom had a few coats.

The host – a flight Lieutenant Davidson sat next to him very politely.

He was the only officer, and on Christmas duty. The fire was lit and the fireplace gave great warmth – he began to feel relaxed. The deserted dining room was spartan, cold even, no one was on base. Soon he led Falcon down a passageway to the officer's rooms – the wall paper was patterned.

'We have the heat on, for your arrival Sir.'

'Thank you.'

'We will soon have Chef, rustle up something to eat and drink.'

'Great,' I nodded.

'You have me checked in.'

'Yes Sir.'

Falcon looked at his watch, it was past midnight

'I have a few calls to make.'

As soon as he left Falcon dialed RAF Leuchers

'Duty station controller please?'

There was a pause.

'Sir, your identity, please,' said the voice.

Falcon gave him his name and rank.

'Speaking from the RAF mess.'

'I see Sir.'

'Can you give me a station duty officer, please.'

'Sure.'

When he came through – Falcon explained that a jet had been scrambled to guide him.

He listened – then said – 'Yes sir, lucky we were operational at that time – that was Wing commander Rogers sir, from RAF Lakenheath, from the US Air force.

Falcon was absolutely surprised, what a coincidence, that someone should have rescued him, who was also American and based at RAF Lakenheath, where he was due to return in the morning and set off back to the States.

'I see,' he said politely.

There was a pause – where is he now.

'He has signed off Sir – he had to go someplace fast – before returning to Lakenheath.

Falcon took a deep breath, the American had gone back to his base, and yet he did not recognize the name at once.

'Splendid,' Falcon said at length.

'It was a marvelous bit of flying – by the wing commander.

'Yes sir, these chaps are up on all kinds of weather.'

'Yes, manning stations at night – at Christmas must be lonely. Happy Christmas.

Falcon put the phone down and sat back and breathed deeply.

REST

He had acknowledged that he knew – and that the American wing commander was no longer available.

It began to dawn on Falcon that he owed his life to a senior officer of the USAF – who had left and dropped everything to get him out of the mess he had found himself in.

'Thank you Sir, Happy Christmas to you too.'

Falcon put the phone down, sitting down in some bewilderment. The radio, compass, fuel; all in one night and it was indeed a night, he would not forget in a hurry. Luck could not come in bigger slices. An ace had found him and quick thinking controller.

Bobbing up and down in the North Sea was not his idea of fun.

He poured some whiskey and quietly raised the glass to him.

The young Flt Lt put his head round the door.

Sir, here is your meal enjoy. He departed with friendliness and cheer.

'Many thanks for your help,' Falcon shouted.

He took his meal and ate heartily. The room was warm – he stepped off his flying suit and put on some pajamas loaned to him.

After his meal, he made a few quick notes in his diary and filled in his log book. His eyes darted to an entry he had made in Syria – he had jotted some notes down on his last mission. It was on Syria and President Bashar Al Assad. He quickly read the notes and closed his diary. He sighed, yes Assad had come to power upon his father's death in the year 2000, and many inside and outside Syria held high hopes that the popular young Doctor, would bring long awaited reform, and that he would be a new kind of Arab leader, capable of guiding his country to genuine democracy.

Many still believed Assad's country under his leadership, although it had seen turbulent times, would survive. There were sporadic reports about his transformation from a great bearer of hope to a reactionary in a national emergency. Rebels had risen, and terrorists groups like Jabhat Al Nusra had corrupted the lands.

The country had become repressed and was inexorably slipping into violence and despair. He was not sure how Syria and the entire region would fare, in the future, he had done his bit for his country, and this was his last mission, before leaving the US Forces. He knew, he would not look back in regret.

He could not have elected for a more lovely evening and after a hot bath, he toweled himself and was ready for his bed. There would have to be some changes, when he got back to Lakenheath in the morning. He would fly out from Edinburgh. Suddenly he could hear eager, voices, the sound came from the dining room downstairs, and the clatter of plates and cutlery began and the place came back to life.

He was soon dozing off.

RETURN TO LAKENHEATH

Falcon woke up sharp at 7 a.m. He was supplied with clothes and flying overalls – if he needed one. As he was ready to leave, the junior pointed out the picture of the wing commander to him – there was something about him, that was very familiar, he knew him, but could not place from where. He had a strong presence about him, even in the picture.

He took long strides and crossed over to the yard and straight onto the car park where a van was waiting for him. There waiting for him was an RAF aircraft ready to fly him back to Lakenheath, he did not have to resort to civilian aircraft after all.

The whole thing was clear as day – he was a fine pilot who had flown with the best crack squadrons in the Middle East– he would no doubt have met him personally and professionally some place. He would like to thank him. He had spotted his triangles and his position with pin point accuracy. He would trace the man once he was back at Lakenheath. He was an exceptional pilot, the best perhaps. He probably had eyes like a cat in the dark, through that fog, he had to be an ace. It would be disastrous to lose one's life in a fog having taken the enemy fire and other things besides in the heat of so many conflicts.

He could imagine him, someone who was quite a giant, a larger than life character.

He turned and watched the fields, the snow had melted.

He met the pilot and shook hands and he nodded gravely. Falcon smiled, 'Merry Christmas and thank you.'

'You too. Sir?'

'I hear you are flying back to the US soon with your team.'

'Yes once I make sure all the jets are in good fit after this episode.

'I am sure they will be Sir – just an unfortunate one off incident.'

'I hope so.'

Soon they were heading back to the base at RAF Lakenheath. He made some mental notes for the long journey home that awaited him. But first he must find the wing commander.

WING COMMANDER

Rolf Metz Rogers was the right man – Perkins and Forrest and Andy Rowe introduced him to the man, the Wing Commander, a second generation pilot and a trained geologist; both factors equally important in aviation.

'Great to meet you, Sir,' Falcon said shaking his hand 'heard a lot about you from the guys.'

'Greatly exaggerated, I can assure you, I am glad we found you as quickly as we could --.'

'Yes Sir – that was a quick, a good thing too.'

'How was your stay at the Mess?'

'Good, they gave me food, water, air and a room with a view – hot bath did the trick.'

'Yes – that is good to hear,' said Rogers with a charming smile..

'We have all been personally chosen for our intelligence, wit or some other redeeming virtue,' quipped in Perkins.

FLIGHT TO US- AIRBASE

Rowe was in charge the next morning conducting pre-flight checks with Perkins.

Like all the inhabitants of Lakenheath RAF base, Falcon would remember this place for a very long time.

Rowe could see that Falcon and Rogers were now alongside the tanker and slowly four other jets swung harmoniously alongside.

Moving into gear, Rowe signaled to them, and then he soon eased into the flight, flying away from the control tower and flew beyond it.

Suddenly the general alarm rose, one of the Jets was in trouble. His reaction was to contact control immediately. Rowe swung into action.

For Christ's sake, he thought it is Rogers; Wing Commander's Jet was going off in a crazy manner.

He could hear him talking calmly to Control – an icy calm that sent a chill up his spine.

The safety procedure was always to move as quickly as possible away from the tanker and other Jets and if possible to land or eject in a place away from built up areas.

Falcon had seen it too, he was horrified. He wished he could do something, should he contact base, just in case, there was a mechanical or radio failure, like his the day before.

LOSING THE EAGLE

Soon Falcon lost sight of Rogers Jet. The light of the sun was streaming in, painting strong patterns of shadow across the cockpit. The unwavering beams of light then moved off with a steady sun beaming.

Falcon stared in utter disbelief as they moved forward.

Suddenly the radio flickered into action – then came the strange and moving words, with horrific emotional content from the Captain – 'Officer Rogers has gone, he died after ejecting moments before the aircraft crashed near RAF Lakenheath Base.'

Then there was silence, everyone taking in the shock of a loss of such a supreme commander.

'We are diverting to Lossiemouth.'

There was more silence, was it a terrorist attack or sabotage?

Falcon thought they are taking no chances.

The sound bites carried on with instructions, and short pieces of news and development. Calm descended on the team.

'The Cambridge constabulary has advised for safety,' came the commander's curt and clipped voice.

Again there was silence, the crew dejected, at such a tremendous loss.

'There were a few refueling problems – he managed to avoid the houses before ejecting.

They flew on there were no more messages.

'Rogers followed procedure, and avoided the houses, before ejecting, the delay may have been fatal,' Rowe came in with a quick comment. Then there was silence.

Falcon was speechless, he was dazed – he could not comprehend, that the man who saved all those lives and lost his. It took him some time to take in the implications of his final act, before he absent mindedly swung his jet into a new direction trailing swiftly behind the tanker.

The curtain for Rogers had come down; the fog waves had found him, taking his life in brilliant sunshine. Roger, the man, and Roger the commander of the skies.

How ironic, that he had saved his life by his skillful deployment with such controlled command and precision. What moral Falcon wondered could he possibly draw from this? He looked down on the fast fading Lakenheath, hiding beneath some tattered blanket of clouds for protection against the vagaries of space.

FLASHBACKS

A few days from now, he hoped to cradle his first son in his arms – what stories would he tell him?

Rogers Metz was down below somewhere not having fallen far from his Jet, but truly he was now far beyond the stars. Falcon reminded himself that for ordinary pilots, two things were important – loyalty and respect – and Metz had both in abundance. It was a privilege to have made his acquaintance.

He was sure he would soon return to Lakenheath again and pay respects to this fine fast Jet Pilot, and consider why he had indeed been truly saved. Soon they would land in Lossiemouth.

ESSAY TWO
GARVOCHLEAH – ANGUS

This short essay is dedicated to the happy ending of the life of a Helmand Province veteran nicknamed "Joe"

INDEX

CHAPTER ONE - AFRICA

CENTRE OF A RIVER

Scotland was beautiful this time of the year. The rivers were growing wider and fuller– Douglas was sure that Ambrose would be waiting for him, once he returned from his sailing trip. It had seemed like a thousand years or more. Then he spied far away in the distance with his binoculars what looked like a galley being rowed down the centre of the river. He had made sure they had guns on board; Africa was notorious for pirate boats. It was then that Major Douglas Phillips went below. He had to be careful for wherever they anchored, there were thieves who would steal anything they could sell. Douglas was not below deck for long and he brought up some guns and pistols. He handed one to the Captain of the ship who took it from him, without any comment. 'I hope you know which of your men are great shots?' The Captain smiled and nodded.

CHAPTER TWO – GARVOCHLEAH

MOBILE -AMBROSE

Douglas Phillips was driving his super-fast mobile. He thought the horsepower was the best he had ever handled. The car was the best acquisition he had made. It was an immensely expensive vehicle and extremely easy to drive. The rearwheels, the floor of the body, its trimmings, its outer sleek form was almost space age – just the way he liked it.

Douglas's high flier arrived once he had returned from the Army, having served in Afghanistan and from his sailing trip in Africa.

He considered it a very sporting vehicle, any gentleman could possess it – it lent itself well on a dual carriageway and it was built well. It was safe and robust. The young officers and women found it alluring.

The vehicle attracted all the fashionable ladies of society to gaze at him insolently especially at the horseraces.

Douglas never felt like a royal but he was conscious of his importance and position to them. He was undoubtedly sure that his return from the war, made him a bit of a mystery, and sought after, smartest guy at the club, but to the frivolous and rich he was just another show off, like the rest of them. Most people still respected the Forces, but most people had, had enough of an unending war.

On his return from Africa, he had taken London by storm. He had received two of the most prestigious medals for his gallantry that the Prince Regent Duke of Cambridge shire, could award. He had praised him highly to the Queen, where he was a constant visitor to Buckingham Palace.

In addition, Douglas was extremely rich, not only because his father had left him a vast estate and fortune but equally because his mother was a great heiress.

All his close circle of friends admired him but there were others who hated him for his wealth, good looks and vast fortune.

To crown it all, his royal connections and being a wealthy heir, perhaps added to the attraction. His success with the beauties of London's elite class made many a man envious. It was his easy grace, charm and above all sincerity that drew them to him like a magnet. Douglas managed to maintain his sense of humor, and keep his sobriety intact amongst the peers of society.

His peers enjoyed inviting him to events of endless gaiety and festivity in London upon his return. The parties had truly begun and were in full swing. The conflicts had lasted more than a decade and it was time to relax. The events were full of sophisticated young women, who would fling themselves into his arms. His fame meant it was not surprising that he for a while courted the most beautiful and talented women. Life seemed perfect, easy exciting but also extremely dull in many ways. The predictability of high society with their mores and rituals lacked a sense of the unexpected and equally purpose.

He was almost 29 years old and it was time to get married. The finest houses in Scotland and England had begun to seem dull and dreary without a suitable companion. Garvochleah had been in the family and George Hall too as far back as the 17th century.

George Hall had been pulled down and a new mansion was being built. His favorite haunt was however Garvochleah, where he found the pleasures of fishing and grouse shooting, very pleasurable. He had in the meantime, given his family house in England to his brother Owen.

Douglas had been brought up in George Hall and he had loved it more than any other place – but now it needed to be rebuild by one of the finest architects – Roger MacDonald. His genius came from the old school of architectural thought – which originated from the era of

Roman renaissance and had principles of formality and dignity in its frameworks producing some of the greatest British historic places and homes.

Douglas however professed a more contemporary modern approach, less formal and moving, rather than rigid in structure and correct in form.

At George Hall, the same architect had achieved this in abundance, although traditional features like magnificent staircases and domes were still part of the impressive feature, the unique marble halls were supplanted with more interesting, open welcoming contemporary features.

When the house was done, it was even more beautiful than before but less imposing and far more welcoming.

Douglas had made up his mind, and moved quickly with his plans. After his father's death, he began to live at Garvochleah, he needed someone bright who would bring the place to life and share his inheritance. Society ballrooms and dances were full of great people of distinguished backgrounds. Ambrose Bancroft was one of them, the daughter of a diplomat.

She was admired, popular and Douglas was struck with her from the moment he set his eyes on her – he knew he was not in love but her beauty surpassed the sculpted goddesses of many a marble hall. He wondered if he should propose to her and what her answer might be. She was used to receiving compliments and no doubt had many admirers. Douglas was not worried. At the next dance he would propose.

The next dance came and went, Douglas could not summon the courage, he decided to walk her home.

'I have a question to ask?'

Ambrose just laughed.

He joined her – her laughter was infectious. It was inevitable that many a man, had done the same - walked her home. She turned around and smiled bewitchingly, almost sensing what his question might be.

'Why don't you join me and my parents for the weekend – this Saturday, I am sure they will be delighted to have you around. Douglas did not say anything – but hesitated, smiled and said, 'I will there at 3 0'clock, if that will be alright?'

'Sure.' she said.

Then to her surprise he did not say another word and politely wished her goodnight and left.

When she settled in her home, she knew, she had won over all her friends. She finally had Douglas's attention.

GARVOCHLEAH RESTORATION

Douglas drove his car with an expertise which was exceptional like everything he undertook.

He was wondering, if the wedding should be in Scotland and honey moon there or elsewhere.

Garvochleah, needed a great number of improvements and some restoration. The House had been neglected for a while. He would invest some money in the restoration of some of the main rooms and get the outside brickwork repointed and granite stone sand washed.

So much to do, Douglas told himself. There would be no time to get bored. Ambrose could entertain as much as she liked there.

He realized the neighbors were friendly and would inevitably call on him when he established himself there. There were no private racecourses there to build and social life would come to a standstill, compared to the hustle bustle of England. Yet there was a guaranteed peace and solitude in Scotland, which was missing in England. Upon his return he had found England especially London overwhelming in every sense of the word. There had been a pile of letters on his desk unopened when he had arrived. There were some invitations and some bills. His secretary had taken care of most things while he had been away. Douglas was sure he would soon be able to put all his affairs in order.

His horses had been well trained and looked after and he would gather speed to have them moved up to Scotland.

They were worth every penny he had spent on them. They were such a joy to behold and equally to ride.

As he turned into the drive of the elaborate gates of Garvochleah, he felt certain; this would be his main place of residence. Punctuality was one of his virtues and he knew someone would be expecting him in a few minutes. The House was vast and opulent and attractive. As he pulled his car to a standstill, he got out and ran up the stone steps to the front door. He rang the doorbell. A Butler opened the door.

'Good morning Sir, I do trust you had a pleasant drive from London.'

'Yes very pleasant indeed.'

The Butler smiled.

'Glad to hear, that Sir.'

He led Douglas a long way, along a furnished passage, without saying anymore and opened a door at the far end. The door led to a room which was decorated with flowers.

Ambrose had already arrived ahead of him, to give him a surprise – she had arranged it with the butler. He had cancelled the appointment to visit her parents at the last moment.

Douglas caught her at the window, where she was looking at some pigeons below. He walked towards her and she held out her arms.

'I was afraid, you would not be in today, Douglas!' she said.

'You knew I was coming – I must say you look tired, you are well?'

She smiled and said, 'It was the drive up here, I only arrived a few hours before you.'

'I see and the reason?'

'The reason, is to find out what your question would be, you cancelled at short notice – worried I had annoyed you.'

'Douglas looked surprised, and then murmured, 'Oh that, was not important, I have forgotten what it was now!'

Ambrose's eyes twinkled.

'I have never known someone as intelligent as you to forget so simply – it must have been important.'

'I will try to recall,' he murmured.

'If it was important I am sure, I would have remembered – however you are here now.'

'Indeed!'

Douglas still had a small box which contained a blue sapphire diamond ring, but he was unlikely to ask her now. She was prone to playing games, and he would wait for someone who would match their superlative quality.

Ambrose gave a little coy, smile after she had distanced herself from him, after giving him a ring.

'I thought,' she said in her deep voice, 'We could spend some time together.'

Douglas stood facing her and said, 'I am sorry Ambrose, I am on business and have very little time – we could have a meal together.

For a short moment, she was astonished at his reply.

'I see, a meal will have to do then!.'

Douglas thought to himself, 'I cannot marry you, nor can you accept this beautiful ring!.'

Almost reluctantly he held his hand out to her.

'You do understand.'

'Yes, it is quite clear – you have a lot on your plate.'

'So it is alright with you.'

'Yes let us take a walk in the garden.'

She was finding the conversation completely incomprehensible.

It had never occurred to her for an instant that he would cool off so quickly, she knew intuitively he was going to ask her to marry him.

As they were walking, she said, 'It may come as a surprise to you, but she continued hesitatingly – but I have promised to marry Dan Shaw.

For a moment Douglas thought he had not heard her correctly – but he knew he had. Dan Shaw was the most unattractive person he had ever known.

Most people considered him a pest as he would force himself on acquaintances who did not want him in their company and then roar in a high pitched voice about all manner of grievances and ills. Everyone found him a bore, and Douglas knew the reason why she had committed to such a bore, and unprepossessing one at that.

Then almost as she said it, he could see the headlines, Dan Shaw to marry Ambrose Bamford. With a rich American background, and being an American senator - Dan Shaw was made of millions and Ambrose loved him.

Now as he stared at Ambrose, he smiled.

She stammered incoherently.

'Douglas I am glad you are so happy for me.'

'Yes I am indeed,' he exclaimed. 'He is wealthy and will keep you in the style you have been accustomed to – you will be loved in the lap of awesome luxury!'

Ambrose turned away from him.

'I hope you understand, he is not as rich as you think and is only a normal rich American – I am not marrying him for his money nor that he is a senator. He is a very special person.'

Douglas drew in his breath.

'I hope for your sake, you have made the right choices and will be eternally happy.'

She could sense the slight sarcasm in his voice.

'Ofcourse, I must extend my congratulations to you both.'

He bowed and took her arm and began to walk her to a waiting door keeper of a posh Scottish restaurant.

As the guard pulled the door open –Ambrose gave a little cry.

'Wait Douglas – I want to talk to you.'

'About what may I ask?'

He led her into the restaurant quietly – they sat and talked.

Once they had reached, back at Garvochleah, he strode her to a waiting car. The butler was no longer there – then he walked purposefully back into the house, up some carpeted steps while, she drove off down the drive. He thought he heard her sobbing as he glanced out of the window. It was difficult to believe things had moved at such a quick pace. How could this be possible? She was beautiful, charming and knew she had fallen for him but could not resist American power and fortune, he could never giver her. Douglas felt sad, surprised, but not horrified or angry. He was annoyed but people married for such superficial reasons. Nobility, wealth and rank had its lure. Deep down Douglas had always been an idealist, where affairs of the heart were concerned.

STABLES – HORSES
AND CAIRNS

He had adored his mother, a sweet and lovely person and had adored his father equally. He thought everything she did was perfect and if they had ever disagreed with each other, it was never in front of him. He had been spoilt by both his mother – they had given him a sense that the world belonged to him and he was superior than anyone else.

He had done well at school, and after Gordonstoun had been a success in the story. He was brought up to believe in himself and that he was an exceptional person. They had died while he was away in the Army. His mother, first and shortly after his father. He had felt utterly alone and now he was on his own but strong and independent. Ambrose had revealed her greedy, grasping, snobbish side and he was a good judge of character. He would just have to wait for the time when the true love of his life to reappear. It was not going to be Ambrose of that he was now certain.

Her engagement would soon be announced and he had escaped certain death. He would visit them, he had always instructed his men in the face of the enemy to fire the first shot – it had made them win many minor and major victories. He had fired the first shot and may have been saved from public humiliation.

She would now be nearing the turn onto the main road to London, aware that she would be most upset at his never asking that one mysterious question that so plaqued, her mind for so many weeks.

He examined Garvochleah, before locking it and headed off into the nearby small villages with their many graceful cottages.

As he came to a fork, he noticed a young man walking aimlessly by. He opened the gate, and walked towards him. Then there was a large iron gate, with a lodge on either side.

This was the home he was seeking and drove up the drive. A very attractive Lodge appeared, to the left although it was very dilapidated. The cracking windowpanes and tiles missing from the roof – the only thing that mattered that his horse had arrived in good working order. The second Lodge was similar.

He pulled up outside the front door and could hear horses neighing amid sounds of their young. He had arrived at the right place.

He walked up the steps – the front door was slightly ajar.

He knocked loudly with his fist. There was no response – he knocked again and a girl appeared – she looked like a lost soul. He noticed her clothes were shabby, she looked unkempt.

She looked surprised.

'Sorry to bother you,' he began, 'but my horses, two chestnuts, Antigone and Equss were meant to have arrived here a few days ago?'

The girl smiled.

'Ofcourse, they have been groomed and are in the stables, follow me,' she added assertively, much to his surprise. He had judged her too soon, and harshly.

She walked down some steps with Douglas steadily following him.

'Your horses are exceptional, you must be very proud of them,'she continued.

'Yes, I hope they were brought safe from London.'

'Yes ofcourse – they like it here.'

'Yes, it would seem so,' Douglas aired his comment.

They reached the stables and a groom came running out.

'This gentleman's horse, Benjamin,' said the girl, 'Can you show him where they are.'

'I will have a look, Miss,' he said.

The girl did not reply but he noticed a hint of anxiety on her face.

It told Douglas things were difficult for her here. Benjamin led the horse from the stables into the stable yard.

The girl turned to Douglas. 'If you would leave me alone, with my horse.'

He suggested –'perhaps you could bring me a cup of tea that would be awfully nice?'

'Sure, right no trouble.'

'She ran off into the house.'

Douglas inspected the horses, and talked to the groom for a while.

The groom checked, the horses had instinctively become energized by the sight of their master.

He made a gesture with his hands, beckoning to the lad, it was alright for them to be returned to the stables under his charge.

Douglas noticed that the garden in front of his house was unkempt too and full of weeds. Brambles mixed in with the flowerbeds. He said nothing as they walked back to the house.

The paper was peeling and the carpets were threadbare.

Several pictures hung and they looked like expensive antiques.

Morag opened the door, and took him into the dining rom.

'I will fetch the tea,' she said.

He realized the house must have once been extremely attractive.

There must be hardship, for it to fall into such a state. Some time passed before she returned with a tray on which lay a silver teapot, milk jug and two cups. She sat down and poured the tea.

'Sorry to be such trouble,' Douglas said.

She simply smiled.

'Do you live alone?'

She shook her head. 'No my brother Benjamin lives with me.'

'Where is he at the moment?'

'He is a good groom.'

She smiled again, looking petite and sad in a strange way.

Douglas moved towards her and sat next to her on the sofa.

'Now tell me, how is business here – do you need help with advertising?'

Morag made a little gesture with her hands.

'Sure, we are in a sorry plight – at the moment. With the recession, people are grooming their own horses; the wages have suffered a bit – over the last three months.'

She stared at him, fiercely as though resenting her weakness and shielding a wounded pride.

'I will see what I can do to let my friends around here know.'

'She drew a breath.'

'Very kind of you.'

Douglas paused and asked her for her card. She rushed and got him one. Her surname was Morag Cairns. He wondered if she knew Mathew Cairns and she exclaimed he was her cousin.

'Mathew is a great pal of mine; we were in the same house together at Gordounstoun.'

Morag stifled a sob, giving a scream as an exclamation.

'You know Mathew.'

'Of course, I do, he is a great friend of mine.'

'Well I am sure that will help.'

Douglas reflected on her story it was a quite unique to find someone like her in these parts. The war had a devastating impact on people all over the English countryside and the recession from the wars had made things worse.

Many farmers and country folk had tried to keep their heads above water.

The British government had tried to help with subsidies, but it was not enough. Life has its usual ups and downs, but these were getting more frequent now.

'Tell me more,' he asked her.

'Well that is all there is to it.'

'And how about you.'

'Well I was almost going to propose tonight – but she had gone for an unpleasant rich man – I would not have been good enough for her.'

'Gosh, that is awful,' exclaimed Morag.

'I feel awful.'

'It is life – she was a power seeking girl, or is.'

There was an awkward silence. He paused before adding
'Could you make sure my horses are fine for a while till I return.'
She smiled.
'No doubt, they will be fine.'
'Why do you say that.'
'Because I am sure they will be.'

'Well, you are right, Morag, but I wonder it might be better for you to advertise your goods at a do in London – you could escort me?'

'Morag turned away, I don't think that is very funny – she said shortly.

'It is not a joke,' replied Douglas.

LAUGHTER

Morag laughed.

'You mean it.'

'Yes, I do.'

'Really.'

'Yes really.'

'What about my horses?'

'You could find someone for a day- I will pay for him.'

'But that is impossible.'

'Why?'

'Seriously.'

'Yes, seriously, you could do a great deal with the estate in the house – once you get more clients.'

'Of course I could – alright then.'

She drew in her breath.'

He was thinking of some of the most dangerous missions, that he had undertaken – he was successful because of keeping things secret.

She thought it great opportunity; it would save the estate and everything with it.

She walked to the window – and looked out at the garden once full of flowers now only weeds.

Douglas knew how important this was for her.

She turned around.

Mathew will be here soon.

'Leave it to me – I can be convincing when something important is at stake. As far as I am convinced this is very important

Morag smiled.

She did not speak.

Douglas continued.

'I plead with you – please.'

She knew he was being sincere.'

'Alright if you are certain and you will guide me – then I will do it.'

'Thank you very much – you will not regret it – I swear.'

He suddenly thought of the velvet box with an engagement diamond ring.

He opened the box and held it out.

He gasped, 'Why it was beautiful, 'he thought quietly

'It would have to fit perfectly, nothing less than perfect would do.

'It quite became her,' he mused quietly to himself, then laughed loudly.

She laughed, too seeing his delight.

She knew nothing of the world outside all she had was her dilapidated house and neglected estate and her stables.

She was totally unaware of how beautiful she truly was.

Perhaps at the right time, she would find someone who would love and marry her.

This visit to London with a total stranger– and what if Mathew objects.

A second later, a man entered.

'Hello Morag.'

'Hello Douglas?'

'Good heavens, when did you arrive here.'

'Oh a few weeks ago.'

'Delighted to see you.'

Douglas laughed.

'Mathew looked at Morag.

'I expect you remember Morag?'

'Well she is the reason for my visit.'

They all laughed.

'Yes, Mathew I will have to explain a lot of things to you, one day. For now, suffice it is to say, we have to head off for London tomorrow.'

'To London,' Mathew exclaimed 'whatever for Doug?'

Morag slipped out of the room.

She listened for a moment and heard Mathew speaking.

'This has taken me absolutely by surprise – I must say.'

'I understand Mathew; you have had a difficult time. I am not running away with your cousin, but taking her out for a day or two.'

'But you cannot do that yet,' Mathew said quickly.

'Why is that, I can and will – we have been friends for a short time but you can trust me.'

'Should I Douglas.'

'Yes – you should.'

'Truly.'

'I know Morag is up against a wall and needs a leg up – don't you think.'

'Your help?'

Morag was listening and got a little perplexed.

She hoped he would not tell her cousin everything.

'So?'

'You have returned from the war and want to restore everything in a day for yourself and others.'

'I can hardly convince you of that but that is how it is going to be' Mathew chuckled.

'Yes you can chuckle but I have a lot of changes to make around here.'

'What way?'

'Well firstly get my horses up and running. I will have to spend a lot of time around here —— you understand with Morag and Benjamin's help.'

'I see.'

'And then there is Garvochleah, it could do with a little feminine touch. Morag could help me restore it.'

'And neglect this place, hardly likely.'

'They are thorough breds and will need riding a lot.'

'And who may I ask.'

'We will have to loan them out to youngsters in these parts – of course.'

'I guess that is one way forward.'

'I know no one could be a better judge and they could enter local horse shows and countryside feats.'

He put his hand on his forehead, as if not being able to take on all of his plans at once.

'I know you are despairing, but you should relax!'

'It is just that you are trying to make so many changes at once.'

'Well if you think I am moving too fast, I can always slow down.'

Morag had heard most of the conversation – the important parts – there was no mention of any engagement. Douglas was now focusing on his horses and revitalizing his grand mansion.

She rushed to the paddock, and Equss came galloping towards her. She took him to the stables and then locked him in safely. She returned to the other stables and began to admire the perfect team. The groom would feed and inspect them in her absence. She walked slowly back to the house. Douglas's horses would be fed well.

The two men were still in deep conversation, as she uttered they ceased speaking.

'Are you coming with us? she asked her cousin.

'No afraid not – I will be here holding fort, while you go on your little excursions.'

Morag murmured, she thought she must check what she would wear.

'Douglas will be staying the night, we must make him comfortable.'

'Any ducks? asked Morag. 'I have a last bottle from last month.'

'Don't worry, a bite to eat, might nourish me back to health?'

'They all laughed.

'Mum was good at this – she said as she rushed off.

'She heard them talking again.'

Morag realized by the way he spoke of his parents, his mother meant a great deal to him – and she would probably be horrified at that cruel beauty – but of course he had not humiliated himself by asking her hand in marriage.

Douglas knew Morag had been absolutely wonderful, by jumping to his suggestion with quick eagerness.

He was thinking how much he wanted to save the stables before they were closed due to financial problems.

He wished she would be able to look after the best horses, it never crossed his mind that if they both walked together, this could be a real possibility and it would make him very happy to make this venture succeed.

Meanwhile Morag knew the first thing she must do is to find suitable clothes – something smart, but her clothes were all packed away. She quickly ran to the drawing room and returned, with a full meal which she laid out on the dinner table. She felt embarrassed as they both sat down to eat and ran away from the room.

Douglas mused - she was an exceptional person, intelligent and quite adorable in her own way.

Back in the kitchen Morag, was making notes of everything the housekeeper would require while she was away. She left it pasted on the fridge door.

The village shops had most things and Mrs Addison had always helped her when she was away. Douglas was just like an Archangel who had descended straight from the highest heavens.

She was happy, she could help him out at his London do – she suddenly thought of her mother's fabulous blue gown worth a thousand pounds – she would wear that one.

They would never starve again, they had been through real tough times twice, that would be the last one this time. With Douglas here, she knew their troubles were over.

Douglas thought she was like ambrosia – a gift from the gods but managed to keep his thoughts about her to himself.

She finally found the evening dress – it was simple yet very elegant. She would take some trouble with her hair. It would be worth taking a few more of her mother's dresses, incase Douglas decided not to approve.

Douglas was stunned by her dazzling beauty, when she appeared in the room, the transformation was complete.

Morag could imagine the many medals on his evening coat. Quickly they were heading off to the airport to catch a flight for London.

EXHILARATION

Driving away, Morag was filled with a sense of wonder and exhilaration. She felt like she was leaving for a novel adventure and waiting for her was all the love, joy and excitement that life could muster.

Douglas had insisted on making sure that his horses were in perfect condition, and that Benjamin had all that he required – before heading off with Morag on a romantic mission.

Morag understood his concerns but he had nothing to worry about, the horses were in very capable hands. Benjamin was equally an experienced horseman. He could handle anything and he rode with much the same expertise as Douglas possessed himself. She watched the stables and waved to Benjamin with sigh of relief, till soon both the stables and Benjamin were lost out of sight.

'Now we must relax Morag, I have given Benjamin enough money for the horses also for his helpers. You do not need to worry while we are in London – they have enough to feed the horses for a month.'

Morag turned around and put her hand on his arm and smiled with kinship and gratitude.

'You are so kind.' Douglas was embarrassed, well she had worked her fingers to the bone, now it was her time enjoy herself and see the bigger and wider world.

Douglas smiled at her.

'Now all you have to do is be vain and glorious – and enjoy the Londoners and live their day! Hopefully it will not be too much of a strain.'

She wondered quietly if he still thought of Ambrose. It may be a hard act to follow – especially when he introduces them casually for the very first time. She hoped, she would not have to meet, the ravishingly beautiful Ms Bamford.

Morag had a great deal of trouble of finding suitable attire for such a grand occasion. Her mother's wardrobe had been untouched till now. She hoped the attractive blue gown of taffeta silk would do nicely. She could recall her mother wearing it to the races and also for dinner parties in the neighborhood.

Her hat was a matching blue silk with pink flowers that went with it.

Morag had never bought fashion magazines, for she did not need them. Her horse riding and stables clothes with an odd pretty dress had been sufficient for her needs. The local pastor's wife was quite vain and superfluous and would insist on Morag having hers. She had latterly given up in total despair – seeing her lack of interest in the subject.

Morag realized that gowns had become less elaborate and flowing than they had been previously. She had therefore selected the least elaborate costume. The Londoners might not approve, but her mother always insisted becoming comfortable with who one is – is the best fashion statement.

Douglas watched her reflecting and wondered what she was thinking. She wondered what good clothes can do for a person, the London dressmakers were famed for making the most fabulous and glamorous garments.

'It all sounds so exciting,' Morag said in a cheerful voice. She had done her best and she hoped he would not be disappointed in her. He made her laugh and kept paying her compliments.

Douglas was ruminating on much the same essential subject matter. He had decided he was going to propose to her and get it advertised in the press. He hoped she would say yes. Of course Ambrose would be there too, and if the Senator and she married it would make all the papers. There were always people like her who knew exactly what they wanted and how to go about it. He concentrated on his driving and said nothing more.

Morag was happy staring at the passing green fields. She hoped no one would notice her much at the Ball, when they reached their destination. She could be quite content in her own company and her own world, she was sure he would not embarrass her by making any grand revelations of any kind that would shock the delights of her evening.

Douglas was well aware, she was anxious yet grateful for the trip.

He concluded she would be alright with their charade. He decided to stop and pick up some drinks and a bite to eat to refresh them.

Douglas enjoyed the brunch and let Morag grab some coffee. She was accidently hungry and soon in a couple of hours they would be on the outskirts of London.. As he moved smoothly through the traffic, he was glad for once he had a silent companion.

'I must say Morag, you are very good travelling companion.'

'You mean because I am silent, sure it is much nicer enjoying the view then you can concentrate.'

'Thanks, he agreed. I hope you have had a comfortable journey.'

'Yes I was just thinking how turning up at this grand house will seem,' and she gave a little gasp.

'It is a very impressive mansion – although it was rebuilt and altered several times – I think you will find it a beautiful building.'

Soon, they were driving up a drive only for her to discover it was even more spectacular then what she had believed. They were greeted by two smart livery men. Douglas helped her out of the car.

'I hope you like the house – it is one of the finest in London – part of the family heirlooms.'

'A handsome present, Douglas and I am sure you are grateful for it.'

'I assume you – I am and thankful for it,' he replied jokingly.

'She was overawed by the grand entrance hall with its exquisite paintings on the walls.'

Two footmen and a butler took their suitcase, coats and hats.

Douglas asked them to serve lunch as quickly as possible and they were asked which drinks they preferred

Morag was amazed how quickly the meal was served and without any commotion.

'I will bring the champagne in Sir,' the butler said, 'in the study and will be through with it in a moment.'

Morag was taken upstairs to the most divine bedroom she had ever seen. There were carvings on the ceiling and glittering gold leaves on the poster bed. There was warm water; she washed her face and hands.

There were maids who brought in her trunk.

'Thank you,' she said.

She hurried downstairs, only to find in the study, everything was polished, shining and elegant. There were fresh flowers on the tables and the sunshine was bearing through the windows shining on exquisite statutes on the mantelpiece.

Douglas in the meantime, had already rung his friend to make an announcement of his engagement in the papers. He had asked it to be posted in the Monday papers. He gave him only skeletal details. His friend showed little surprise at the news.

'I am thinking,' Lieutenant Todd his friend enquired 'Of asking for a photo of you two – if I may?'

'Of course that can be arranged – he said.'

When Douglas had supplied him with a photo of them with the horses in the background, Todd had exclaimed it was a most beautiful and natural picture he had ever set his eyes on and congratulated him on his splendid choice.

From then on the Todd knew exactly what Douglas wanted. He also handed the Lieutenant a list of shops to arrange a trousseau and thanked him.

Morag had no idea, expensive dresses were being ordered for her from Drury lane.Todd – sent out his secretary and she accomplished it in a few hours – the instructions were clear and the money was ample.

Todd marveled at the beauty of his fiancé – by far the prettiest girl he had ever seen, she also had an ethereal look about her – something totally missing in the famous London beauties. It was at first glance a beauty of a different kind. She appeared shy- he knew he would be soon introduced to her, as he had been invited to the house by Douglas.

'Todd,' Douglas was saying, is my best man, a genius at everything.

'That sounds wonderful,' said Morag

She was thinking of her own house where ceilings fell off and chimneys got blocked and drains froze.

'Thank you, added Todd, I was prepared for the unexpected.

He watched as Morag was looking around the study.

'It is a very impressive house,' she said politely.

'Indeed it is,' replied the Lieutenant.

'It takes time; it is so breathtaking, 'Morag,' he said, let me show you the portraits of ancestors and what the decorations on the table are.'

Morag was thinking, this was wealth beyond her little feeble imagination.'

Lunch was great – and she needed a rest till dinner was served.

Todd continued, 'let me show you the library and where all the books are stocked'

'It is very up to date.'

Todd showed her the library and entertained her, while she chose some books and decided she would read them. She thanked Todd and Douglas and put on her dressing gown – and lay down to rest. She had hardly read three chapters when she fell asleep. The excitement had worn off. She dreamt of the horses and Douglas and people who were very successful. In the dream, she felt lost bewildered and helpless. She could not contribute anything to these people while they spoke to each other in laughter and jest.

She was not aware, when it was morning. She made an early note of all that she had been shown the night before, pictures, antiques, silk and books.

Most of all, her curious nature was such that wanted before anyone else to be aware of what was happening next.

Douglas was still waiting to surprise her – and was hoping the engagement would be announced as soon as possible after he had proposed to her.

He decided to call his friend Mathew in Scotland. He knew it was not a very long and drawn out affair and they had only met – but he was sure and sensed her admiration for him, even love – a love at first meeting.

'I heard you have arrived in London, Douglas, I am delighted to hear from you.'

'Yes, Mathew, I have something of a very personal nature to discuss with you. I wonder if you could shut out all distractions for a few minutes.'

What he said instantly intrigued him and he put down his newspapers.

'What are you doing at the moment?'

'Well I was heading off into the garden if you should know – to join the others – it can always wait.'

'You have company.'

'Yes, but it is only the horse crowd.'

'Well.'

'Now just you tell me Douglas? I am impatient – do proceed.'

'This may come as a surprise to you –Mathew but I shall be proposing and announcing my engagement soon after.'

'What' –there was excitement in Mathew's voice.

'It is not that Ambrosia Bam ford is it? There has been gossip among our friends.

'No, in which case they will be disheartened?'

'Who is it?'

'But everyone is certain it is her.'

'I know, Mathew but I am about to be engaged to the most beautiful girl in the world in London.'

'Someone new – this is wonderful tell me, I am all ears!'

Mathew threw the question with an eagerness which was totally uncharacteristic of him. Although he was getting old and going fat, but he still had the joy of life and people found him totally irresistible in his older years.

'Do go on!' he said seating himself comfortable.'

'Are you sitting down Mathew, should I start at the very beginning?'

'Yes, who is this beauty no one has been allowed to see.'

'Well – you will have seen her.'

Mathew was delighted.

'Ofcourse, ofcourse!' he said.

'She is one of our common friends from school or university.'

'Not quite.'

'Well you have not yet told me who she is; Mathew persisted.

'I expect you may be horrified – if you remember a Cairns family – her father commanded the British soldiers in Gibralter.'

Mathew was silent for a moment.

'He died a long time ago.'

'Mathew knew what was coming next.

'His wife died shortly after as you know.'

'Yes,' Mathew said.

'It is their daughter!'

'I am proposing to take her as my wife.'

'An old respected family –their daughter.'

'You approve then.'

'Morag – that is good Douglas, very good.'

'I had hoped that is what you would say, she is your only niece and I thought I should ask you first.'

'You have my blessing – just try not to frighten her while she is among the critical members of your society.'

'I will try!'

'It will be interesting to see their surprise and also irritation that they have lost an eligible bachelor to a country girl.'

'Yes it would be most amusing.'

Mathew chuckled as he was well aware that they all waited to remain in the inner circle.

Douglas said, 'Alright Mathew, I have to go is there anything else you would like to add.'

'No Douglas I must not.'

Keep me informed what lies ahead.'

Douglas paused before he added.

'Yes, now Morag and I have to face the critics, hopefully they will not find too many faults.'

He knew that Mathew was pleased, and he had not hesitated to express his joy.'

'Ok, Mathew,' he said.

'He heard him chuckle as he replaced the phone.'

Douglas thought of Morag, and how easily bored she got. She was used to living in the country, in a huge house which had once belonged to her father. There was a great deal to be done He drew in a deep breath, and thought of what lay ahead.

Nothing could possibly upset Morag now, once she was introduced, the majority of them would follow his lead.

As he was thinking, he realized there was one vital issue he still had to cope with, that Morag would remain her confident self in company. She would be out of her comfort zone. She was like a dramatic heroine stepping onto a stage for the very first time, with her background she would be fine. He was musing when Morag appeared – she looked pale, tired and very anxious.

DOUGLAS PAPERS

Douglas was ready and waiting. He waited reading the morning papers. Douglas thought she looked lovely at dinner the previous night, at dinner in a pale pink floral jumper and dark trousers.

He had never met anyone like her – she did not talk incessantly about herself or flirt like the others. All she did was ask questions about Garvockleah and he was delighted to tell her about his favorite project. She kept the conversation going and they had a few arguments about its history.

It seemed like she was catching up having been alone with her brother and overpowering and imposing cousin Mathew. Her father cropped up a lot in her conversation, her horses, the estate.

Her laughter was infectious when her eyes lit up with memories of her glorious past. She was totally absorbed in the world, in an intellectual way and probably found talking about herself a dull subject.

Douglas thought there was a way about her, that was refreshing.

He decided to tell her about the war and the distinguished people he had met, from all over the world. She was sharp on Foreign Ministers of most countries but admired only a few.

It was strange how quickly dinner was over, it was almost half past eleven.

'We must go to bed Morag – you have to look your best tomorrow – and catch up on your beauty sleep – no nerves, no dark circles, no last minutes anxiety attacks – promise?'

The lines I think that is very unlikely at my age – and I will draw the curtains tight,' she laughed as she spoke then added.

'I would like to thank you for everything you are doing for us – it has been a while since I have experienced such overwhelming kindness there are no words.'

'Morag there is no need – it is my pleasure to have the company of one such as you – the pleasure is all mine.'

'Oh yes!'

'No worries about tonight, you will outshine them all, you always do.'

'Good night!'

He opened the door for her.

She dropped a curtsy, then laughing ran off in the direction of her bedroom.

Douglas thought she was more fun than anyone he had met.

When Morag returned to her room, she quickly undressed got her night pajamas' on and climbed into a very comfortable bed.

'Thank you Dad, thank you Mum, she prayed over and over again and fell fast asleep.'

Douglas hurried to breakfast the next morning, demanding to see the papers. He had just finished breakfast – when Morag appeared with a collection of clothes with the housekeeper, carrying some on her arms.

Douglas was amused. He decided to sit in, and watch with his usual flair, the boudoir that had been unleashed from Morag's bedroom.

She paraded each gown in turn – it was like a mini fashion show, with him along with his minimal staff the only audience.

He asked his butler to take all the calls and to let the callers know he would be in London in the evening.

He was in the meantime, curious to watch Morag's choice in clothes.

He had never seen so many clothes being paraded – the attendants were generous as usual.

His long discussions made him aware her knowledge of history and politics was as good as his, and if he dared admit – better than his.

Her love of reading was obvious.

He remained seated comfortably in his leather armchair – while Morag continued her parade.

'Voila! – another one!' she cried

She suddenly walked towards him in an extremely full evening gown it was glamorous, spectacular and dramatic.

The bodice was crossed over in blue and the high waist had a matching emerald green sash – the shirt was fine muslin embellished with flowers and a truck of lace and velvet. The neckline was modest and not low but very stylish and elegant. Although the dress was very attractive, Douglas shook his head. It was too elaborate more for stage than a ball.

Douglas could hear a heated argument between the housekeeper and her. It was like playing dice or a game of billiards.

He waited patiently for the next show up.

Morag returned in a gown made of soft material – woven silk in blue which gave the impression of moonlight – when she moved. It was ordinary in that it had no decoration on it. There were some trimmings at the bottom of the dress – in lace, but no flowers, or ribbons.

The gown was Morag's mother's which she had already decided she was going to wear this one; she had to convince him it was the one. Her gown was flattering in every sense of the word.

Douglas did not say anything, but clapped his hands in excitement – as he knew this was the one that was finally perfect.

Morag smiled as though she had won a great victory over her audience and her sole spectator and bowed with a final flourish.

She ran and sat down in a chair beside him

'Gosh I am exhausted!' she exclaimed. Douglas put his head on her forehead.

He chuckled.

'Yes that was quite a parade for the day!'

'I never realized looking the part can be so exhausting a bit like galloping around the grounds at hundred miles an hour!'

'Morag you have only just started, the event, has not even started.'

'You are a hard task master.'

Douglas realized she was innocent – the country life suited her – the city could be so destructive in so many ways.

It was time for lunch and they both decided to continue their conversation at lunch.

Later the bath had been made ready for her. The bath water was sprinkled with oil of lilies and then the hairdresser would arrive. He arranged her hair – in a most exquisite manner. Anthony the hairdresser was amused; he had never come across such an obedient client with not a touch of spite in her, unlike the other famous ladies. She was a creature who had arrived from a faraway land. He was bursting with curiosity now. After she had arrived he had been astonished by her presence and gentle grandeur.

He was an artist and knew exactly how to accentuate something special in his client. He brushed her hair till it shone, then he had arranged it in the latest fashion. Douglas would be surprised. He was sure of what he had created. As he left, Anthony met Douglas.

'Signore, tonight the ladies will be jealous.'

Douglas smiled; Morag did have something of the Greek goddess about her.

Douglas wished to see her. She was there sitting feeling shy and demure, at odd with her new look.

Anthony had used his brilliant talent – she was looking elegant and the hair do made her beauty breathtaking.

'Anthony is a genius.'

'Morag's eyes sparkled – he was pleased.

'So, what? She said and bowed.

'The jewellery and the gown – you will be glittering like dewdrop on roses – like diamonds in the sun.'

Morag rushed up and got dressed, Douglas knocked at her door.

'Come in,' she said.

'I have something for you.'

'Oh Yes?'

'Well.'

In his hands he held something he was hiding.

'Turn around.'

She did so obediently.

He clasped a narrow necklace of diamonds and sapphires around her neck.

Then he placed a similar bracelet around her tiny wrist. He slowly took out the blue sapphire diamond ring, and placed it on her finger, it as he expected fitted her finger perfectly.

'Morag dear, will you marry me?'

She looked at him stunned and smiled and said simply 'Yes, I will Douglas, dear.'

'You will be the belle of the ball.'

'Oh gosh.'

'Yes, you are in for a real treat.'

She took a final look at herself in the mirror.

For a moment there was total silence in the room.

'Now we must leave!'

'Thank you Anthony,' she said.

Morag held her arms out and he kissed her gently on her left cheek.

Then they both went downstairs while Anthony still amused, knew tonight was when he too had reached a new light of brilliance with her – something, that had eluded him before.

Driving towards the house, Douglas remarked.

'I wonder who will be there!'

Morag laughed she was totally at ease.

'As they arrived at the Mansion, there were many cars parked already.

'I am sure you will enjoy every moment of it.'

'How many guests do you think?'

'Around two thousand invited.'

Morag gave a cry of disbelief.

He pressed her hand gently.

'I will love to see the inside of this grand house.'

'Yes, we can see it at some appropriate time later.'

They walked along the long staircase, he took her tiny hand in his – he could see she was trembling a little.

The Prince was receiving the guests. He was an exceptionally handsome man and genially welcoming his guests. Diana would have been so proud, had she lived to see him grow. He had his mother's easy manner.

'I have been waiting for you, Douglas,' he said.

'Thank you your highness – may I present Morag Cairns.'

Morag bowed a shallow curtsy.

The Prince looked happy.

'Lovely meeting you,' he said.

'He took Morag's hand in his and led her in.'

'They will all love you my dear.'

'Yes, Sir,' she said politely.

'How did Douglas find someone as glorious as you – in the depths of Scottish country?'

'His horses are in my charge your highness,' she replied.

'Perhaps it is called fate?'

The Duke laughed, she was witty, sharp and confident.

'So that is how you met.'

'Yes Sir, he is my neighbor – having returned to Garvochleah after the war.'

'Well actually, your highness I have known her since she was ten years old – her cousin happens to be one of my best friends.'

The Prince was amused and clapped Douglas on his shoulder.

'Well done, Douglas.'

As more guests appeared, he moved away from them.

'Well Douglas, Morag and you will be sitting next to me at dinner and so he departed.

Douglas was thrilled and overjoyed as was Morag.

They gradually moved into the drawing room, and everyone rushed towards them.

He could see Morag was a hit and they wished to make her acquaintance – a new beauty had suddenly arrived for them out of nowhere.

She accepted the compliments and knew how to evade probing questions.

In the dining room, there was a large table and several others – smaller ones to accommodate all the guests. There were beautiful flowers sprinkled with diamante.

Douglas noted that Morag's diamonds glittered in the light of the rooms.

There were tiny lights hidden amongst flowers – and scenic effects managed very carefully.

'It is so beautiful here, your highness,' Morag enthused.

'Yes, I am always trying new things.'

'Such a marvelous house.'

'I shall show you around myself,' he suggested, 'If you would like that.'

'I would love to your highness.'

'There are a few goddesses in her chamber – marble ones of course.'

'Morag was delighted to be paid such a marvelous compliment.

Douglas caught sight of his many friends. Suddenly Colonel Tom was waving to him from across the room. He slowly began walking towards him, while Morag conversed with her new found friends.

His civilian friends had kept asking him why and how he had devoted his life to such a terrible period of history and it was indeed not much of an answer to say there had been worse. Journalist's reports on Afghanistan could only give brief glimpses of the reality on the ground. The full story of what happened in the operations - Athena and others; the combat missions with battle groups engaged in a deadly multiple year war to counter insurgency in Kandahar province, was quite something else.

Morag seemed to be enjoying herself finally relaxing in this company. He was happy to leave her on her own. Tom was immersed in conversation, but looking his way.

He could hear others discussing Afghanistan fervently. It was an unprecedented combat and besides a battle, there were many active operations, military and psychological and Afghanistan was probably the longest most complicated and challenging operation of the Middle East. It was in the end a humorless heartache for many. With Iraq commencing soon after, it soon became a forgotten war, with all eyes turning to Iraq.

For over 2,500 years, the forbidding territory of Afghanistan had served as a vital crossroads for many civilizations. History had shaped it well, with influences from Greek, Arab, and Mughal, Civilizations. The Mughals had their rule there, followed by other great empires.

He watched as Prince Harry a veteran of the wars in Afghanistan, began circulating among the guests. He was making his way up towards Morag, and soon he was having a conversation with her.

He finally found Tom who looked at him with his commanding and piercing blue eyes. Tom held on to Douglas as though meeting a long lost friend, and for a while not letting him go. Douglas knew, Tom still needed to offload as best as he could.

'Something, that overthrowing the Taliban, in their own country,' Tom said.

'Yes sure, they did harbor terrorists, but soon they were on the run, once the Americans landed.'

'But Douglas, America's initial easy victory did not last long did it?' he stated rhetorically.

'What do you mean?' I asked him in return.

'Well it is in sharp contrast to their securing the state afterwards.' Tom said politely.

'Well, its historic struggles and changing nature of its political authority – have proved it always bounces back in time, yet this time, it seems different somehow.' Douglas added politely.

'I suppose the civilizations before built it up.'

'The Mughals, Greeks..'

'But the Americans, Russians and the brave British,' I said.

'The Taliban resurgences have not helped either.'

'Yes, bewildering diversity of tribes and groups – never could truly grasp how they unite as one nation.'

'Yes, somehow, their regional and cultural even political differences seem not to divide them.'

'Well we were like that once', said Tom picking up a drink from a passing waiter carelessly.

'You mean the scots and the Irish?'

'Well governing these people seemed relatively easy – with power in the hands of small elite.'

'Now?' Douglas asked.

'Well, their delicate political system has been broken before in the 19th and 20th centuries,' said Tom.

'Like Militias expelling us the Brits and later others like the soviets?' Douglas added to the conversation. 'They are a gritty lot, I must say!' said Douglas half laughing.

'They have proved themselves remarkably successful against foreign occupiers, in the past, but….' said Tom not finishing off his sentence.

'What? Tom.'

'It has undermined their own government's authority, making it difficult to govern of course?'

'Sure.' Douglas nodded.

'Their armed factions are still continuously trying to create civil wars.'

'The clerics don't help of course.'

'They are to blame for their own isolation from the world,' said Tom.

'Well I guess we cannot sort the entire world, but the yanks certainly toppled the Taliban, but could not rebuild the country as quickly as they had made it unstable.'

'It is a graveyard for British and soviets, the US could not avoid the same fate, history's lessons.'

'So you are saying it is a failure, in the long run Tom.'

'I could see from the corner of my eye that Prince Harry had concluded his conversation with Morag and was easing his way into other crowds. She was standing there alone with a drink in her hand looking forlorn and awkward.

I quickly made my polite excuses with Tom and rushed off to get another drink.

Soon I was beside my damsel in distress.

Morag thought of Mathew, he would never believe this when she would tell him of her trip. Her brother too, she would introduce him to London soon.

'Like an impossible dream unfolding.'

She thanked her Dad quietly. She noticed Douglas was laughing and talking halfway down the table. She noticed a bright light had enveloped him.

It was the heavenly light of the gods – which even the Prince's roses could not conjure up.

'He is awesome,' she said to herself – 'I hope he never disappears – this feels like I am living a dream!'

MUSIC

As Douglas and Morag drove back in the early hours of the morning, Morag talked happily about the evening.

It was one of the best evenings, Morag had ever had.

They had gone into the garden and watched the lovely dancers from outside. The music filtered out, and occasionally they could hear rapturous applause.

The orchestra bowed. It was an entirely novel experience for Morag. Douglas had paused then added.

'Especially for you –'

'Spectacular,' sighed Morag.

'Tomorrow morning, after breakfast a quick round of the relatives or else.

They will think we are ignoring them.'

'Yes, we should do that.'

She had before going to bed, leaned over the banisters and called, 'Thank you – an evening to remember.'

He had smiled and she returned his wave.

Douglas knew the evening has been a success.

He had a long list of all the relatives he had to visit.

Douglas, knew it would take them all the time to see them all. Morag could not sleep – she lay awake thinking of the dancers, the house with its beautiful paintings. She had met such exciting people, who never once asked awkward questions. She tried recalling their faces and names and finally she fell asleep.

The next morning, she had hurried downstairs for breakfast hoping not to be too late. She dressed in casuals, when she walked in, Douglas was eating his breakfast and reading the papers.

'Good morning, Morag, we must leave soon, get you back to Cairns House – the horses will be expecting you.'

'Your relatives?'

'Yes, see a few only.'

She helped herself to bacon and eggs from one of the shelf dishes from the sideboard.

Morag said, 'Yes quick breakfast and home.'

They soon left, walked to the car together and packed their cases into the boot.

Morag stole a last glance at the beautiful mansion. They were on their way to call on his aunt, his mother's sister. She was around sixty years old but quite good looking. She had been widowed and was spending her time raising money for children in need. She had the same charm as Douglas and she could see Douglas in her a lot. They were shown to her drawing room.

'Douglas – I was just writing a letter to you – having read about your engagement.'

'I am sorry – you could not hear in person, it has taken me a long time to persuade Morag. She has said, she liked the ring.'

He kissed his aunt then introduced Morag. 'She is the cousin of the Cairns boy – the one from Gordonstoun.'

'Yes of course.'

'I remember him.'

'You are so like your mother – this is amazing.'

Morag gave a cry.

'You knew my Mother – that is the best news yet.'

'Yes, I would love to talk to you about your mama – she was a friend of mine.'

'Oh.'

Douglas knew that this was good now.

'Aunt, we need your help, we would like to advertise Cairns House to your friends – and as far and wide as possible –

'Yes, I must ask my secretary to assist me via the many charities we support.'

After a good visit, he called it a day and kissed his aunt's cheek. As they drove off Morag seemed sad.

By the look on her face he could see she was thinking of her parents.

She had longed to ask many questions but did not as his aunt was extremely pleased to meet them. They chose not to stay long.

'She is a tiresome woman; sorry it was a brief visit.'

'She was once.'

'Do you really think so – she was nice I must admit.'

Morag laughed – then they travelled on to other cousin's houses – who were mostly pleased that Douglas had decided to settle down.

Morag smiled. She realized all his relatives loved him and were proud of him, they decided to finally head back to Scotland. He could see softness in Morag's eyes and wanted to make a comment but decided not to.

'Why are you so quiet Morag?'

'I was thinking.'

'What?'

'About love.'

'What about it?'

'Love cannot be manufactured.'

'How do you mean.'

'Well love is a mystery, a gift of the gods – it is magical, it comes seeking you, it is far more important than to go looking for it – that is its mystery, anything else would belittle its importance.

'Yes, like us.'

'Yes, like you.'

'My father and mother loved each other very much, when they were together. There was mostly sunshine around them and us.'

Douglas was silent for a moment.

'It is strange – nice to be raised in a house filled with love.'

Her fingers tightened around his.

'We hope to make you happy, Morag.'

Douglas realized she had read Greek classics and the belief system that God created man and then his ideal woman – who was her in all respects – a mirror image.

Her soft gentle, spiritual nature convinced him – that her ideal person was he himself, the other half of herself – which would complete them as one person.

Douglas found it very touching – she was besotted with him and so was he with her.

Douglas gave a chuckle.

They laughed together and finally arrived at a place to dine.

LORDS

Morag and Douglas were driving back and the lunch would have to be brief. He had hoped to take her to dine with the House of Lords but there was not time enough but he would next time. He would keep it as a surprise, his friend had a yacht and he had stayed on it. It was beautiful and one of the biggest and fastest yachts he had ever seen – he had hoped to buy one himself but then had his first passion, his horses.

It was strange he thought that Ambrose had not been at the Ball, nor her engagement to the Senator announced – he was slightly puzzled. She was not one to miss the special parties. He would soon find out from mutual friends. The whole thing was ridiculous. Aristocrats were sometimes the most superficial and dull people who had been given an exaggerated sense of their self-worth – some never achieving much for themselves in their lives – having inherited their titles and their inheritance from their families. The fairytale princess was fast becoming a myth. He was glad one well deserving candidate had been given an experience of a style that was a one off.

She knew Mathew would be making plans for the stables and she could now contribute to this grand design. 'We are so very lucky,' Morag, thought to herself.

Douglas was thinking of the time, Ambrose had invited him to the House of Lords. He had been early. It was usual when one was invited to dine at the houses of parliament in the summer for guests to go in the traditional manner to the terrace and admire the river Thames. The view was attractive – and he could see the boats and yachts smiling past. She had on a lovely dress, and Douglas had thought she looked enchanting. It was ordinary but not ostentatious. When they had arrived at the House of Lords, they had been escorted to the terrace – where the other guests were standing.

Douglas knew her well and General Thomson had been longing to speak to her the entire evening. He knew the general had great respect for him, he was well aware the General was fond of him. Everyone arrived punctually and there were ducks being served. She liked alcohol and often drank more than she should. If he had been sensible, he should have refused that invitation. He would take Morag to see Garvochleah, he thought. He truly wondered what had become of the most wonderful Ambrosia. Soon they would arrive home.

As they unpacked and entered the butler took their cases. There waiting for him in the ante room was Ambrosia.

He could not believe it. He quickly introduced Morag to her; he hoped she would not be rude. He felt uncomfortable and overwhelmed and even embarrassed by her presence.

Quickly he turned to Morag.

'Stay with Ambrose,' he whispered. He then quickly moved away from Ambrosia to avoid any uncomfortable conversations - he knew Morag could handle her.

'Congratulations on your engagement,' he overheard her saying.

'Thank you,' replied Morag.

'My dear, he was an outstanding officer – out in the same hot spot, finding solutions to our problems abroad.'

'Yes I am very proud of him.'

Douglas went outside, and took his day for a quick walk around the grounds, now he knew, she had played a game – one that she had lost – and the pain he had to admit was self inflicted.

He had to avoid a conversation with her at all costs. Hell hath no fury like a woman scorned.

When he got back much to his surprise the two of them were behaving like best buddies and long lost friends.

Morag went to bring some dinner, helped by the chef, playing the kind hostess – she had no ideas of all the viles of Ambrosia.

'I have to talk to you, Douglas,' she said.

'What about?'

'About your engagement.'

'What about it, I hope you are happy for us.'

'Wait Douglas you must listen to me.'

Douglas thought that was a strange thing to say.

'You must be careful she is too young and innocent for you and your wild ways. 'Yes but that is exactly what I want.'

'She is an animal freak, freeing trapped dogs, healing horses – you will be bored with her in no time at all.'

Douglas drew his breath.

He could not imagine that this woman had the nerve – she had returned to ruin his engagement with Morag. Did she have to be so unpleasant and boring. Douglas could feel a fight swelling up inside him – then he took a deep breath, this was stupid – he felt a huge burden had slipped off his shoulders.

Morag arrived. The sight of her, sent a quiver surge through him – he was never going to lose Morag– he vowed silently to himself and left the room.

SILVER

Morag woke up and opened her eyes. She could not remember where she was. She had a flash of terror, she remembered it was a nightmare. She dreamt she was aboard a ship and that she had been abducted but was safe.

Douglas came in and held her in his arms and kissed her. She felt his love sweep through her entire body. She loved him and that was all that mattered and he loved her. He had ordered breakfast for her in bed.

LOGS

Douglas woke up early. He realized he had slept like a log. He had expected Morag to sleep on. When he peered across at her she was still asleep. He decided to go down for breakfast and get ready to take her to the stables and Cairns House. Ambrosia had left leaving a note behind on the desk in the front hall. So much for the concern or lack of it, he thought to himself. She would probably marry her Senator quietly. He noticed a paper laying on the chair it was the morning post on the second page – was the announcement of the engagement of Ambrose to the Senator. He read it carefully and drew in his breath. He was 39 years old and holder of the some special accomplishments and a war veteran– now it would be passed on as the greatest match made in society. Is that what Ambrose had paid him a visit for – he could not be sure. He folded the paper and put it into the waste paper basket.

HOME IS GARVOCHLEAH

Douglas had a wedding to plan and this time it was his own.

He would ask Morag about it later in the day – he felt as if the skies had opened and he was walking into the sunshine with a heaven of his own. He was quite sure that in her own magical way; Morag would get everything she wanted and a great deal more. She was up and came running down dressed. She was unpretentious, kind and he could imagine her with white flowers in her hair. It would have to be in a cathedral. He knew now with a clarity, she was his precious darling, his very own, in a thousand different ways, that he had ever dreamt of, perfect glorious like sunshine, only that this time it was from heaven.

They quickly drove to the stables, locking Garvochlea behind them. She looked radiant and supremely comfortable.

Ambrose had got her Senator – but for him there were many extraordinary things to do. A sudden feeling flooded his soul, like a flame from a fire or light from the sun – it was the spirit of love which had joined them as one completely – they were one person.

He had got Garvochleah, Morag and she had got her ancient Greek story and made it real.

'I adore you Morag my dear,' he whispered in her ear, as the stables neared and he could even from here hear the excited voices of Equss and Chestnut. They knew their master had returned once and for all.

ABOUT THE AUTHOR

The author was born in Kashmir, India, and her father served as an officer with the Eighth Gurkha Rifles with the British and Indian Armies. The author's uncles both served in the world wars. Her paternal uncle was a great influence in her life and served as a naval attaché under President Eisenhower. She married an air force officer and pilot with whom she traveled to many places in Asia, Europe, Africa, Far East, and the Americas.

She primarily trained as a scientist, a molecular geneticist, and conducted research in cell membrane genetics, signaling and transduction systems, collaborating with Jefferson Medical School in Philadelphia, Sloane Kettering New York, and NIH Bethesda.

After obtaining her doctorate, she taught and researched extensively in molecular genetics and biomedical sciences. She entered the legal profession, trained as a lawyer with a highly reputable international firm, and completed her masters in intellectual property law, earning a first with distinction in her dissertation. She later completed a master's course in international relations and politics, which serves as a foundation for many of her books.

The author has two sons, one who is an officer with the RAF married to a British Airways pilot and first officer. The second son is training for a career in aviation as a trainee pilot, hoping to follow in the well-established family tradition, but engages an additional passion for Formula One racing. The author is currently an entrant with the faculty of advocates and college of Justice in Edinburgh, Scotland.

Lightning Source UK Ltd.
Milton Keynes UK
UKOW01n0808180816

280941UK00004BA/35/P